WiLF THE MIGHTY WORRIER

RESCUES THE DINOSAURS

Georgia Pritchett

Illustrated by
JAMIE LITTLER

Quercus

QUERCUS CHILDREN'S BOOKS

First published in Great Britain in 2017 by Hodder and Stoughton

1 3 5 7 9 10 8 6 4 2

Text copyright © Georgia Pritchett, 2017
Illustration copyright © Jamie Littler, 2017

The moral rights of the author and illustrator have been asserted.

A CIP catalogue record for this book
is available from the British Library.

ISBN 978 1 78429 873 9

Printed and bound in Great Britain
by Clays

The paper and board used in this book are
made from wood from responsible sources.

Quercus Children's Books
An imprint of
Hachette Children's Group
Part of Hodder and Stoughton
Carmelite House
50 Victoria Embankment
London EC4Y 0DZ

An Hachette UK Company
www.hachette.co.uk
www.hachettechildrens.co.uk

WiLF THE MIGHTY WORRIER

RESCUES THE DINOSAURS

For my boys

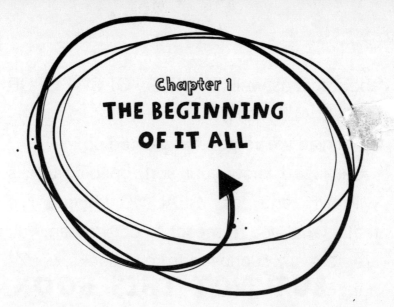

Chapter 1

THE BEGINNING
OF IT ALL

Yes?

Can I help?

Oh, I know what you're thinking. You think this is a book, don't you? You think this is a book with a sweet little story in it, don't you?

Well, you couldn't be more wrong.

I mean, it is a book, yes. I'll give you that. And it has got a story in it, so you're right about that as well. BUT IT'S NOT SWEET OR LITTLE, ALL RIGHT?

I'm glad we've got that cleared up.

Because I know your sort, opening books willy-nilly and just READING things, like that's what you're meant to do. I mean, you are normally supposed to read books, you're right. **BUT NOT THIS BOOK**. Because THIS BOOK is different. This book has a blinking **STAGGERBLASTING** story full of **SCARYNESS** and **SURPRISINGNESS** and **SHOCKINGNESS** and things that there aren't words to describe. Well, there probably are words but I expect they're very long and difficult to spell so I won't be using them.

Think you're up to it?

Do you though?
Do you though?

Do you though?
Sure???????

All right, then. Buckle up. This is going to be quite a ride.

You know Thingy? What's his name? Wilf! Yes, Wilf. That boy at school. The one with scruffly hair and pingy ears and a head so full of ideas it's like dozens of idea-shaped chicks hatching in his brain. Yes, that's the one. He has a little sister called Dot who is sticky and stinky – she's like a tiny smell-making factory who has a grudge against nostrils.

So anyway, last week, right, the world nearly ended. But it didn't just nearly end, it nearly ended before it had even begun! Yes, it did! Oh, there was a great big old kerfuffle, but luckily Wilf saved the day. THIS is what happened…

Wilf was at home, laminating his latest list of worries (as you do).

   This was his list:

skeletons
blood and innards
being eaten
sleepovers
being squashed flat

Meanwhile, Dot was busy being a dinosaur. Dot LOVED dinosaurs. And even though she was little and couldn't say words like 'biscuit' (she said 'bikkie') or 'yellow' (she said 'lello'), she had no trouble saying 'therizinosaurus' or 'ankylosaurus' or, her favourite, 'Tyrannosaurus rex'.

Just then, Wilf's mum wandered by to tell Wilf and Dot that they had their shoes on the wrong feet.

'RARRRRRRRR!' replied Tyrannosaurus Dot.

'Do you want to go to the museum to see the dinosaurs, Dot?' asked Wilf's mum.

'RARRRRRRRR!' replied Tyrannosaurus Dot.

'You like the museum, don't you?' asked Wilf's mum.

'RARRRRRRRR!' replied Tyrannosaurus Dot.

'Wilf, why don't you take Dot to the museum to see the dinosaurs?' said Wilf's mum.

Wilf tried to explain that he was a little bit busy laminating and that Dot would be just as happy staying at home watching him laminate as she would looking at dinosaurs, but it was difficult to be heard because Dot kept shouting, 'Zee-um! Zee-um! Zee-um!' every time he opened his mouth.

'All right,' sighed Wilf. 'I'll take Dot to the museum.'

And THAT was where the **whole kerfuffle** started.

Chapter 2

A LITTLE BIT LATER

The truth was, Wilf was a bit scared of the museum. Wilf was scared of skeletons and the museum had a dinosaur skeleton which was ENORMOUS, and he was worried that it would chase him in a **clickety-clackety** way and then **CHOMP** him up.

But Wilf knew that Dot would enjoy the museum. So he got out his '**HOW TO STOP WORRYING**' leaflet.

Number One said:

1) It can help to think of things that you feel thankful for.

Wilf tried to feel thankful. 'I'm so happy that the dinosaur will have such fun chasing me in a **clickety-clackety** way and I'm so pleased that it will **CHOMP** me up because it probably hasn't eaten for a while and so it's probably quite hungry and I know it's a carnivore which means it likes meat and I'm made of meat so that's lucky. For the dinosaur.' Wilf trembled. This was actually making him feel quite a lot worse.

He put away his leaflet and had a great big old worry and then he had a great big old think and then he thought so hard that his brain almost got overcooked and then he had an idea!

He decided he would take something to block out the **clickety-clackety** noise, and that he and Dot would wear their bicycle helmets so the dinosaur couldn't **CHOMP** their heads. And then he would take a jar of Marmite – just in case.

Wilf packed his backpack and took Dot outside to collect his best friend and pet, Stuart. Wilf knew Stuart would enjoy the museum too. Stuart was in the garden sliding down a really, really long straw because Stuart is a crazy thrill-seeker. And also a woodlouse.

Just as Wilf was popping Stuart in his pocket, Alan leaned over the fence. Alan was Wilf's next-door neighbour. He liked to think of himself as the baddest man in the whole wide world. Not a little bit bad by accident, but bigly bad on purpose.

'Hey, you!' said Alan. 'You small mammal things.'

'You mean children?' prompted Wilf.

'Yes. That. You. Guess what I've been doing?'

'Is it something lovely?' said Wilf, walking over. 'Like stencilling? Or making a picture with lentils? Or writing a lovely poem?'

Alan snorted. 'Writing a poem? Writing a *poem*? I hate things that rhyme! They're a complete waste of time.'

'That actually did rhyme,' observed Wilf.

'No, it did not. What absolute rot.'

'So did that...' said Wilf.

'Do you want to know? Or shall I just go?' said Alan, stepping back into his garden.

'And so did that,' said Wilf, looking over the fence. 'I think deep down inside you, Alan, there is a sensitive poet wanting to get out.'

'Don't make me mad! You know that I'm bad!' said Alan. He kicked the fence, realizing that he had rhymed again.

'Now try to pay attention. I've invented an invention,' said Alan, accidentally rhyming *again*. He jumped up and down with frustration.

'It's very, very clever. My best one ever,' he added. He shook his fist at himself.

'The thing is,' said Wilf, 'we're on our way to the museum. To look at dinosaurs.'

'RARRRRRR!' agreed Dot.

'Museums are boring,' said Alan. 'Stop all that roaring!' He kicked the fence again.

'Just come round and see…?' he said sadly. 'There's time before tea.'

Then he took his shoe off and threw it very hard, and it accidentally got stuck in a tree.

Alan looked down at his sock, which had a big hole in it. He gave his toes a sorrowful wiggle and sighed.

'OK, we'll come,' said Wilf kindly, 'but we'll have to be quick.'

Wilf and Dot went back into their house and put their coats on, picked up the backpack, swapped their shoes onto the correct feet and left.

'Zee-um! Zee-um!' said Dot.

'I know,' said Wilf, 'but first we promised to look at Alan's invention.'

They rang on Alan's door.

There was no reply.

They rang again.

They heard a muffled, 'Let's have another go, shall we?' from Alan and a muffled bark from Kevin Phillips. Kevin was Alan's right-hand man, who was actually a dog.

Then there was a sort of whirry zoomy splodgy sound. Then another muffled bark and then Alan saying, **'Get off me! Muddy pawprints!'**

Wilf and Dot rang AGAIN. Finally Alan opened the door. He was covered in muddy pawprints.

'Yes? What is it?' he barked.

'You said to come round,' said Wilf.

'No I didn't,' said Alan.

'You said come round and look at your invention,' said Wilf.

'No I didn't,' said Alan.

'Yes you did. I said about the stencilling and the lentils and the poem,' explained Wilf.

'Then you got cross. Then you kept talking in rhyme. Then you said museums are boring. Then you said to come over. Then your shoe got stuck in the tree and you had a hole in your sock.'

Alan looked at Wilf like he was completely potty. 'My shoe's on my foot,' said Alan.

It was true. It was.

'You are talking absolute nonsense,' said Alan. 'I said nothing of the sort. Now if you'll excuse me. I'm inventing an invention.'

And he slammed the door shut.

How strange! thought Wilf.

And THAT was where the **whole kerfuffle** started. Well, actually it was five minutes *before* it started.

'Well, here we are,' said Wilf.

'Zee-um, zee-um,' chanted Dot.

'At the museum,' said Wilf.

'Zee-um, zee-um,' chanted Dot.

'About to see the big dinosaur skeleton,' said Wilf. He gulped. 'The big dinosaur skeleton that might suddenly come to life and chase us in a **clickety-clackety** way and then go...'

'**RARRRRRRR!**' suggested Dot.

'Precisely,' said Wilf. 'And **CHOMP** us up.'

'RARRRRRRRR!' said Dot excitedly.

'Luckily, I've come prepared,' said Wilf. 'I've brought a pair of your socks to use as earplugs so that I can't hear the **clickety-clackety** noise. I've brought our bicycle helmets so he can't **CHOMP** our heads. And I've brought a jar of Marmite.'

'Yummmmm!' said Dot.

'Yes, I know *you* like it,' said Wilf, 'but nobody else does. And I'm pretty sure dinosaurs won't, so if one comes **clickety-clacking** towards us, we can just rub the Marmite all over ourselves and then we won't get eaten.'

And with that, they went into the museum. Dot rushed around roaring at all the dinosaur exhibits. Stuart stood on Wilf's shoulder, excitedly pointing at things with his fourteen legs. Even Wilf had to admit it was all jolly interesting.

One interesting thing that Wilf discovered was that dinosaurs had lived on Earth for 135 million years. That is much longer than humans, who have only been around for about 200,000 years. That's like saying if time is a sausage, which it quite probably is, humans are the tiny knobbly-bobbly bit at the end. And the rest is all dinosaurs. Or if time is a very long train, there are lots of rows of strange splodgy-slurpy creatures at the front, then about 675 rows of dinosaurs, then just one human at the back.

I don't know why it took us so long to turn up. Although maybe it's a good thing it did, because another interesting thing that Wilf discovered was that the dinosaurs became EXTINCT sixty-six million years ago when a HUGE METEOR hit Earth.

But the most amazing thing of all that Wilf

found, was a cabinet with an isopod in it. It was like a giant Stuart that had lived under the sea a gazillion years ago.

Stuart was thrilled. Wilf was fascinated. Even Dot was impressed. Stuart's ancestor lived in dinosaur times!

'RARRRRRR!' said Dot.

'RARRR!' said Stuart back.

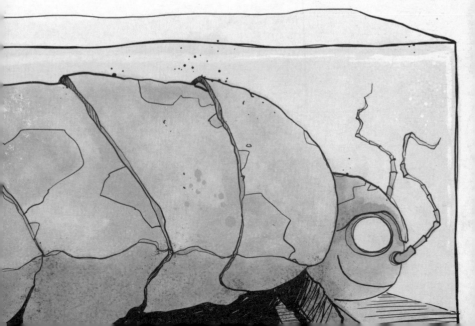

Finally, they got to the room with the big dinosaur skeleton in it. It was huge! It towered above them menacingly, its sharp teeth bared in its enormous skull, the claws ready to strike at any moment and its huge tail curving down to the ground. Although it didn't have any eyes in its eye sockets, it definitely seemed to be watching Wilf.

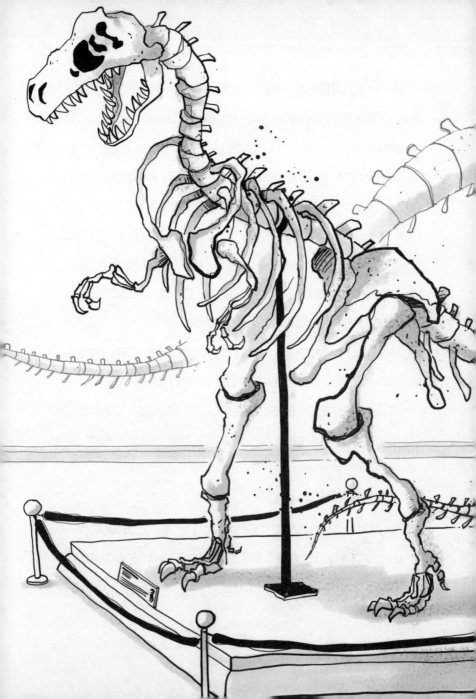

Wilf clutched his jar of Marmite tightly and bravely read the information below the skeleton.

'The Tyrannosaurus rex, often known as a T rex. Tyrannosaurus means "tyrant lizard" and rex means "king". This is because the T rex is thought to be the king of the dinosaurs.'

'Excuse me,' said a muffled voice. Wilf removed the socks from his ears.

'If the T rex was king of the dinosaurs, who was king of the humans?' said the voice.

Wilf turned around. The voice belonged to Alan. He was standing behind them (no longer covered in muddy pawprints).

'RARRRR!' said Dot.

'What are you doing here?' said Wilf. 'I thought you said museums were boring?'

'No I didn't,' said Alan.

'Yes you did. Earlier. When I said about the stencilling and the lentils and the poem,' explained Wilf. 'Then you got cross. Then you kept talking in rhyme. Then you said museums are boring. Then you said to come over. Then your shoe got stuck in the tree and you had a hole in your sock.'

Alan looked at Wilf like he was completely potty. Again. 'My shoe is on my foot,' said Alan.

And it was true. It was. Still. Again. Wilf was getting very confused.

'Who was the king of the humans?' repeated Alan.

'Well, there wasn't a king,' said Wilf, 'because there weren't any humans.'

'Really? No king? Hmmm. That gives me an idea…' said Alan.

But before he could say any more, there was a loud barking noise. They looked round and saw Kevin Phillips bounding towards them.

'No, Kevin! No! Bad boy! I said wait outside!' shouted Alan.

Kevin had spotted something. Kevin had spotted several somethings. Not just one bone. But lots and lots of bones. And not just little bones, but giant ginormous bones. And bones were one of Kevin's VERY FAVOURITE THINGS.

Kevin launched himself into the air, tongue

lolling, tail wagging, ears flying. He clamped his jaws round the end of the T rex's tail and waggled his head ferociously. The whole skeleton started to wobble!

Wilf, Dot and Alan were standing at the front of the dinosaur skeleton. The shaking from the back of the skeleton made the whole thing lurch forward and begin to **clickety-clackety** towards them.

'**Aaaaaaaaaaaaaaaah!**' screeched Wilf. He wasn't wearing Dot's socks! He could hear the **clickety-clacking**! His worst fear was about to come true and they were all about to be **CHOMPED**! Quick as a flash, Wilf put his bicycle helmet on, put Dot's helmet on, then opened his jar of Marmite and slathered it all over himself, all over Dot and all over Alan.

The **clickety-clacking** stopped. The shaking stopped.

But then Wilf heard a loud sniffing sound... Kevin Phillips sniffed so hard he let go of the bottom bone and plopped to the floor with a gentle thud. He lifted his nose and sniffed harder. Because if there was one thing he loved *more* than bones, it was Marmite.

Suddenly Kevin located the source of the delicious smell and bounded towards them. He launched himself into the air once more – and landed on Wilf, Stuart, Dot and Alan in a huge hot fluffy wagging heap of licking and woofing and slobbering.

'Kevin! Kevbthhhin! Geth off me!' gasped Alan. 'Thhtop! Thtop! Yuk! Thtop it thith inthtant!'

Kevin did exactly what Alan said. AFTER he had ignored him and licked every single drop of Marmite off everybody first.

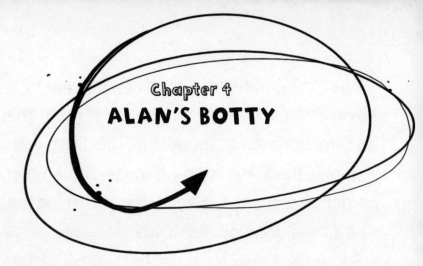

Chapter 4
ALAN'S BOTTY

Wilf, Dot and Alan lay in a soggy heap. The good news was that they hadn't been **CHOMPED** by a dinosaur skeleton. The other good news was that they were no longer covered in Marmite. The bad news was that they were rather slobbery.

Wilf dried Dot and himself off as best he could with Dot's socks. Then, while Alan slurped home with Kevin trotting waggily behind him, Wilf took Dot to the museum shop.

The museum shop is an excellent place to calm your nerves if you've been chased by a dinosaur skeleton or half licked to death by an evil baddy's right-hand man. It's also good if you just fancy picking up a couple of knick-knacks.

Wilf, Dot and Stuart spent ALL their pocket money. Wilf bought a very interesting dinosaur book with lots of pictures. He also bought a T-rex cuddly toy, which wasn't scary at all, and some dinosaur chewing gum. Dot bought a tiny T-rex costume, which she put on right there and then. And Stuart bought a dinosaur yo-yo and a dinosaur pencil sharpener.

Then they all headed happily for home, excited to play with their new toys.

Just as they were getting home, Alan rushed out of his house, stopping briefly to fall over Kevin Phillips.

'Quick! I've invented an invention! It's my best one ever! Come and look!'

'But that's what you said earlier,' said Wilf.

'No I didn't,' said Alan.

'Yes you did. When I said about the stencilling and the lentils and the poem,' explained Wilf. 'Then you got cross. Then you kept talking in rhyme. Then you said museums are boring. Then you said to come over. Then your shoe got stuck in the tree and you had a hole in your sock.'

Alan looked at Wilf like he was completely potty. Again. 'My shoe is on my foot,' said Alan.

And it was true. It was. Still. Again. Again!

'So will you come and look?' persisted Alan.

'Well, all right,' said Wilf.

Wilf, Dot and Stuart followed Alan into his house.

'Behold!' said Alan grandly. 'I have invented THIS!'

He swept a sheet away to reveal a big cupboard. With a sort of clock on the outside of the door.

'It's a cupboard,' said Wilf.

Alan looked deflated.

'I mean, it's a jolly nice cupboard,' added Wilf quickly. 'And it's a very shiny cupboard. I LIKE cupboards. I'm a fan of the cupboard. I bet you can store lots of useful cleaning products in there...'

'It's NOT a cupboard!' exploded Alan. 'It is something MUCH BETTER than that. I call it my Box Of Time Travelling Through Years – or my **B.O.T.T.T.Y** for short. Who wants a closer look at my **BOTTTY**?'

Wilf and Dot couldn't help giggling.

'What?' said Alan angrily. 'What is it?'

'Nothing,' said Wilf.

'BOTTY!' shouted Dot. It was one of her favourite words.

'Drat! OK, forget that, forget that. I shall

call it my Box Of Orbiting Back Years – or my **B.O.O.B.Y** for short. Who wants to see my **BOOBY**?'

Wilf tried very hard not to laugh.

'What?' spluttered Alan. 'What now?'

'Nothing,' said Wilf. 'That's a very good name.'

'BOOBY!' shouted Dot.

'Drat! Drat! OK, forget that, forget that. I shall call it my Special Machine for Exploring Lands Long-ago. Or my **S.M.E.L.L.** Who wants to experience my **SMELL**?'

Wilf tried to wipe his smile away with his hand.

'SMELLY! SMELLY! SMELLY!' chanted Dot.

Alan sighed and massaged his temples.

'Why don't you just call it your **Time Machine Thingy**?' suggested Wilf.

'Good idea!' said Alan. 'Now, it had a few

glitches this morning so I could only travel backwards and forwards by five minutes. It was very frustrating!'

'Oh!' said Wilf. 'So *that's* why you had one shoe and then you didn't have one shoe. And you had muddy pawprints and then you didn't have muddy pawprints.'

'Anyway, I have unglitched the glitches and now it works. So, who would like to time travel with me?'

'Um, no thank you very much,' said Wilf, politely.

'NO!' shouted Dot, less politely.

Wilf could sense that Stuart didn't think it was a very good idea either.

'Come on!' said Alan. 'It will be fun. And it almost certainly won't turn us inside out like it did to the banana I used as a test run.'

'Um, no, really, we're fine. Thank you, though,' said Wilf, very politely.

'NO!' shouted Dot, much less politely.

'What about if I told you I was going to travel back in time to the age of the dinosaurs and meet real dinosaurs and become ruler of all the dinosaurs and all the world?' said Alan grandly.

'That's terribly kind of you,' started Wilf, but before he could finish, Dot shouted, 'DINOSAURS! **RARRRRRRR!**' and toddled into the **Time Machine Thingy**.

'Dot!' shouted Wilf. 'No! Stop!' and he ran in to get her. Quick as a flash, Alan and Kevin Phillips jumped into the **Time Machine Thingy**. Alan locked the door, set the clock for a squillion gazillion years ago and pressed the big red **GO** button.

And a squillion gazillion years ago is where the **whole kerfuffle** REALLY started.

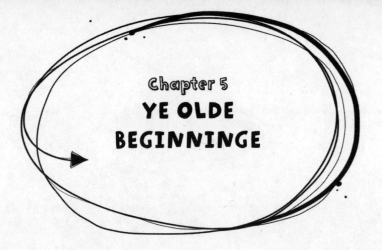

Chapter 5
YE OLDE BEGINNINGE

Well, I don't know how often you've travelled back in time to the Late Cretaceous period, but I'm sure you know it is a rather bumpy plummetty spinny twisty ride. And Wilf hadn't had time for a wee. He hadn't had a wee at the museum because he didn't like using loos when he was away from home. And he hadn't had a wee before he left home for the museum because he was too busy swapping his shoes and Dot's shoes around. So the last time he had had a wee was – well, by the **Time Machine Thingy**'s clock – about 500 years ago!

'Alan!' said Wilf. 'I really need a wee.'

'No time for wees,' said Alan.

'But I really, REALLY need a wee,' said Wilf.

'You should have thought of that earlier,' said Alan.

'The thing is,' said Wilf, 'I don't want to have an accident in your lovely **Time Machine Thingy.**'

'Good point,' said Alan. 'All right, we'll stop. But just for five minutes.'

Alan moved towards the **Time Machine Thingy** controls. In the middle of the control panel, there was a huge shiny metal globe with lots and lots of levers on it. And then there were hundreds and hundreds of coloured wires all connected to another clock. The hands on the clock were whizzing backwards so fast they were a blur.

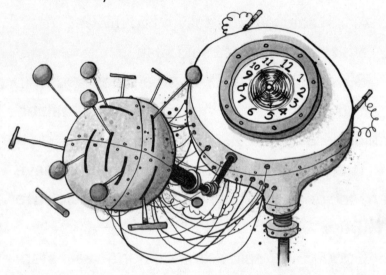

Alan put the brakes on. There was a loud squealing and creaking and then a sort of whirry zoomy splodgy sound and then the **Time Machine Thingy** came to a halt with a big BUMP!

Wilf opened the door and peeped out. He saw a beautiful garden and some pointy trees and a huge maze – it all looked rather familiar.

'Where are we?' said Wilf. 'And more to the point, *when* are we?'

'According to the clock, we're in the year 1546,' said Alan. 'But I'm not sure where.'

'Hang on, I know!' said Wilf. 'We're in Hampton Court Palace! I've been here before on a school trip, and although I'm not a fan of loos when I'm not at home, these ones were really quite acceptable.'

Wilf and Dot and Stuart and Alan and Kevin Phillips stepped out of the **Time Machine Thingy**.

Suddenly, they heard a commotion. **'Off with her head!'** bellowed a very loud voice.

Wilf peered round the corner. He could not

believe his eyes. There, standing in front of him, was Henry the Eighth. Yes, Henry the actual Eighth! I know! Incredible, isn't it? Henry the blinking old Eighth. Unbelievable really. Almost like I'm just making all this up. But no, there he was.

I expect you want to know what he looked like now, don't you?

That is so typical!

All right then, just this once, I'll tell you.

He had a really really really big red face. But in a very royal way. And he was really really really tubby. But majestically tubby. He was dressed, head-to-toe in very clanky armour. And he had a big bushy, fiery-red beard that moved around when he shouted. And he shouted a jolly lot so it was a very busy beard.

Above his busy bushy beard was a cross-looking nose, fierce-looking eyes and ferocious-looking eyebrows.

'**Off with her head I said!**' thundered Henry again.

'Whose head?' asked Wilf anxiously.

'My sixth wife. Catherine Parr,' roared Henry. 'Come on! You strange-looking peasants can come and watch.'

'Um, the thing is, we're a little bit busy. We're just on our way somewhere. Or some*when*...' said Wilf anxiously.

'I, King Henry, am ordering you to come and watch this execution!' thundered Henry. 'And after I've chopped her head off, I'll probably pull out her gizzards and use them to do some skipping or something.'

'SKIPPING!' shouted Dot excitedly.

'Jolly good,' said Alan. 'That sounds very evil and I love evil things,' he added, but his voice was a bit more trembly than usual.

Wilf's ears went all hot. And he felt sick, but just in his neck. And his knees wanted to bend the wrong way. Wilf was scared of blood and gizzards and squishy things like that.

Wilf wished he was at home knitting or whistling or hopping or all three at once, but he wasn't, he was here and he was about to be faced with a lot of blood and gizzards.

And on top of that, skipping, which he didn't like either (mainly because he was no good at it).

Wilf had a great big old worry and then he had a great big old think and then he thought so hard that his brain had a coughing fit and then he had an idea!

He would use Dot's sock (even though it was still a bit slobbery) as a blindfold so that he didn't have to see the blood or gizzards. And if the squelchy sound of blood and gizzards became too much and he felt sick, he could be sick into the big paper bag that the museum shop had put all their toys into. He popped back into the **Time Machine Thingy** to get it.

'Excellent idea!' roared Henry, when Wilf came out again. 'A blindfold for my wife and a paper bag for her head to roll into once it's chopped off!' Henry added, grabbing the socks and the bag from Wilf.

Oh dear.

'Um, could I possibly ask why you are chopping Catherine Parr's head off?' he said.

'Well, I just invented this really good game called tennis,' said Henry. 'And I just served this really good serve. And she said it was out. And I say it was in.'

'That can be tricky,' agreed Wilf.

'And when you have an argument with someone, there's only one way to resolve it,' rumbled Henry.

'What's that?' asked Wilf.

'To chop their heads off, of course!' bawled Henry.

'I'm not sure that's true,' ventured Wilf. 'Isn't it better to listen to both sides of the argument and then...'

'Are you disagreeing with me?' bellowed Henry.

'Er no. That is, I'm just suggesting that there might be another option.'

'No there isn't,' roared Henry. 'Now, have you any last words?' he asked Catherine.

'Yes. The ball was out,' said Catherine stubbornly.

'Right. That's it. Your head's coming off!' thundered Henry.

'Fine,' said Catherine. 'You'll probably miss my head too. You'll probably chop his head off by mistake instead,' she added, pointing to Wilf.

'The thing is,' said Wilf, 'the problem with beheading someone is that I imagine it's awfully difficult to rehead them afterwards.'

'Hmm. You have a point!' said Henry. 'Think I was a bit hasty beheading my second and fifth wives, Anne and Catherine H. Felt a bit bad. I tried to rehead them but the blasted things just kept rolling off again!'

'You see!' said Wilf. 'And if you chop Catherine's head off, you won't have anyone to play tennis with.'

'True, true...' mused Henry. 'Nice armour by the way,' he said, pointing at Wilf's pink bicycle helmet, which he was still wearing.

'Oh thank you! Would you like it?'

'Yes I would!' bellowed Henry.

'Hmm. I'd like to give it to you but it's very precious. It's made of the finest, erm...

plastic and I'd really need something in return,' said Wilf.

'Fine, fine. You can have whatever you want,' thundered Henry. 'A swan sandwich? A horse? A palace? A castle? Name your price!'

'You can keep all your swans and horses and castles and palaces,' said Wilf. 'Because what I really want is for you to promise not to chop any more heads off. Ever.'

'Hurrumph. You're just trying to ruin all my fun,' grumbled Henry. 'But very well, if you insist.'

Wilf put his bicycle helmet on Henry's head and fastened the chinstrap, and then Henry put his crown back on – on top of the bicycle helmet.

'How do I look?' bellowed Henry.

'You look very royal and kingly, Your Majesty,' said Wilf. 'Now, if you don't mind, I need to use the facilities and then we must get back to our **Time Machine Thingy**.'

'DINOSAURS!' yelled Dot.

'Yes, we're going to see the dinosaurs,' said Alan. 'I built a **Time Machine Thingy**,' he added proudly.

'Dinosaurs? What are dinosaurs?' roared Henry.

'You'll find out,' said Alan. 'Well, actually, you might not. They were only discovered in the nineteenth century.'

'RARRRRR,' agreed Dot.

'Absolute poppycock. I've never heard of so-called dinosaurs and therefore there's no such thing!' thundered Henry. **'And I should know, I'm king!'**

Well, Wilf was only gone for five minutes (and by the way, in case you're thinking of visiting, the bathroom facilities in the 1500s are NOT acceptable) but by the time he came back, Alan and Henry were having a huge argument.

Alan was showing off his mobile phone. 'I can play my music wherever I go,' he said, waving it around.

'So can I!' bellowed Henry. 'My musicians follow me round with their lutes and lyres and play whatever I tell them to.'

'Well, I can take a picture wherever I am,' said Alan.

'So can I!' roared Henry. 'The Royal Artist just gets out his paints whenever I tell him to.'

'Well, I can talk to anyone whenever I want wherever I am,' said Alan.

'So can I!' thundered Henry. 'I just send a messenger on his trusty horse.'

'Well, mine is better,' said Alan, sulkily.

'If you don't shut up, I'm going to put a tax on stupid moustaches and then banish you and behead you!' growled Henry.

'Come on, you two,' said Wilf. 'We talked about the whole beheading thing. Let's stop squabbling and leave Henry to finish his game of tennis, shall we?'

And with that, Wilf pushed Dot and Alan

back into the **Time Machine Thingy**, stopping briefly to trip over Kevin Phillips.

And THAT is where the **whole kerfuffle** started. No, but it REALLY IS this time.

Chapter 6
A SQUILLION GAZILLION YEARS BEFORE THE BEGINNING

The **Time Machine Thingy** bumped and plummeted and spun and whirred and zoomed and splodged, and Dot said 'AREWENEARLYTHEREYET?' a million bazillion times – until finally they arrived at their destination. A SQUILLION GAZILLION years ago.

Alan opened the door. They all peeped out.

I expect you're wanting me to describe what it looked like, aren't you? Blooming typical. You know I hate describing things. I expect it looked a bit like things look today. But different.

What do you mean, that's not good enough?

All right, all right! There was grass and trees and ferns and hills and volcanoes. There was a river. The sun was shining. And in the distance they could hear a strange sound.

Hmm? What? You want to know what the strange sound was like too? Do I have to do everything round here?

All right, the strange sound was like the call of an unfamiliar bird. Like a sort of cooing sound but more cawy. Like a cawy sort of sound but more hooty. Like a sort of squawk mixed with a warble. A sort of whistley quack with a cluck thrown in.

Wilf, Dot, Alan and Kevin Phillips stepped out of the **Time Machine Thingy** and then they stopped in their tracks. For there, in front of them was the most incredible sight.

What? You want to know about the incredible sight as well?

This is exhausting!

OK, OK. The incredible sight was dinosaurs.

Lots of them. Huge, enormous dinosaurs. How can I explain what they looked like?

Try to imagine if sheep were green and had really long necks and were fifteen metres high and looked less woolly and, well, I suppose more dinosaury – that is a bit what it looked like.

Try to imagine if cows walked on their hind legs and had enormous scales on their backs and if, instead of eating grass, they ate each other. That is a bit what it looked like.

Try to imagine if chickens could fly and their wingspan was about ten metres and their beaks were really really long and they didn't look like chickens at all – that is a bit what it looked like. Clear now? What do you mean, no?

Well, I've done my best.

'Wow!' breathed Wilf, watching the magnificent creatures moving gracefully across the land, grazing on the grass and the ferns.

'**DINOSAURS!**' yelled Dot, clapping her hands and jumping up and down.

'Gosh. They're biggish, aren't they?' said Alan.

Kevin Phillips lay on the ground and flattened his ears and whined. Kevin hadn't met many other animals except squirrels and cats. He loved squirrels and cats. He especially loved chasing squirrels and cats. But these animals didn't seem very squirrelly. Or catty. Or chaseable. In fact, they seemed quite scary.

Wilf noticed Stuart tapping him on the shoulder and pointing urgently towards the river. There on the riverbank were several large isopods mooching around near the water.

'Look, Stuart! Your ancestors!'

Stuart jumped up and down with excitement.

'And look at that bumpy dinosaur with the big tail!' said Alan.

'Ankylosaurus,' said Dot.

'And look at that big one with the long tail and the long neck,' said Wilf.

'Maxakalisaurus,' corrected Dot.

'And look at the one with the big flat head and three horns,' said Alan.

'Triceratops,' said Dot knowledgeably.

'And the tall one with the really long claws!' said Wilf.

'Therizinosaurus,' said Dot impatiently.

'They're beautiful!' whispered Wilf.

'Yes,' agreed Alan. **'And they're ALL MINE!'**

'What do you mean?' asked Wilf.

'You said in the museum that there was no king of the humans. Well, all that's about to change, because now I'm here. **And I'm going to be king of the humans AND ruler of the world!'**

And with that, Alan got out a little stepladder, climbed to the top and started to address the dinosaurs through a megaphone.

'Behold! Prehistoric creatures, I, King Alan, am your ruler,' shouted Alan.

'No, he's not!' boomed a voice. **'For I, King Henry, am your ruler!'**

They all turned round to see Henry clanking out from behind the **Time Machine Thingy** in his armour and pink bicycle helmet.

'What are you doing here?' snipped Alan.

'I clung on to the back of your **Time Carriage Thingy**. Bit of a bumpy ride to be honest. Think I was sick on a Viking. And someone in a toga. And a pharaoh. Sorry about that. Anyway, thought I'd come and find out if these so-called dinosaurs actually existed. See what all the fuss is about.'

'Go away!' hissed Alan. 'I'm busy being king of the world! Where was I? Oh yes... **Behold! Prehistoric creatures...**'

'Who's he calling prehistoric?' said a spinosaurus.

'I, Alan am here...'

'I Alan? What a ridiculous name!' said a maxakalisaurus.

'I have come to rule over you,' continued Alan, **'as King Alan, the all-powerful king of the world.'**

'**No!**' thundered Henry. '**I, Henry, am better and more powerful than him and I shall rule over you as king of the world!**'

'Who are these hilarious little pink creatures that keep squeaking at us?' asked a triceratops.

'I've no idea but they look quite delicious,' replied a spinosaurus.

'Look,' said Alan, turning to Henry, hands on his hips, 'I am better than you.'

'Oh no you're not!' bawled Henry. 'I have hundreds of horses. How many do you have?'

'I don't have any horses,' said Alan.

'Ha! See!' roared Henry triumphantly.

'BECAUSE I have a CAR. Cars are better than horses.'

'Car? Car? What's a car? There's no such thing as a car! You're just making words up!'

'No I'm not,' shrilled Alan.

'All right, how many wives have you had?' growled Henry.

'One, of course,' said Alan.

'I've had six! Six wives! Six is more than one! And how many castles do you have?' bellowed Henry.

'I have a house. And a holiday caravan,' said Alan defensively.

'I have fifty-five castles!' roared Henry. 'And how many people have you killed?'

'Unfortunately none,' said Alan. 'But I've tried jolly hard and I did scorch some people's eyebrows once.'

'I've killed hundreds. No, thousands!' boomed Henry.

'So what?' said Alan. 'I come from the future where there are laptops,' said Alan.

'And what do you use those for?' bellowed Henry.

'Well, mainly for looking at videos of cats. But we have tablets too!' said Alan.

'And what do you use those for?' thundered Henry.

'Well, mainly for looking at videos of cats. Plus don't forget my mobile phone as well!' said Alan.

'And what do you use that for?' roared Henry.

'Also for looking at videos of cats,' admitted Alan.

'Know what I've got? That's better than that?' bellowed Henry.

'What?' asked Alan.

'Cats!' thundered Henry. 'Actual real-life cats. Which I look at. So I think that decides it. I am **king of the world**!'

'No,' said Alan, stamping his foot. 'I think you'll find that I thought of it first so *I* am **king of the world**.'

'I think you'll find that I am **king of the world**!' said a voice so loud that the ground shook.

They all looked up and there, towering above them, was an enormous ginormous Tyrannosaurus rex.

'He makes a good point,' squeaked Alan.

'Yes, an awfully good point!' yelped Henry and they both turned and sprinted as fast as they could towards the **Time Machine Thingy**.

Wilf scooped Dot into his arms and was hot on their heels, pausing only to trip over Kevin Phillips.

But just as they all reached the **Time Machine Thingy**, the Tyrannosaurus rex's mighty tail swished across the ground and knocked it high into the air, where it somersaulted, plummeted to earth and broke into several pieces with a **CRASH**!

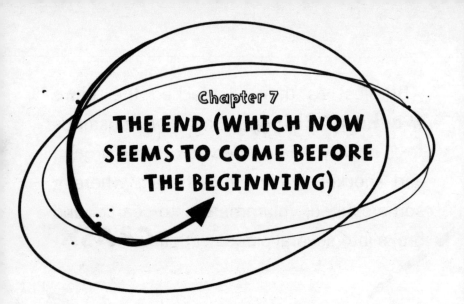

Chapter 7
THE END (WHICH NOW SEEMS TO COME BEFORE THE BEGINNING)

Well, I don't know how often you've been trapped in a prehistoric era with no way of getting home, but as I'm sure you know, it is not a good feeling. Especially if you're surrounded by hungry dinosaurs.

There was a very loud rumbly noise. Wilf wondered if the nearby volcano was about to erupt. But no, the rumbling was coming from the T rex's tummy. He had forgotten to eat breakfast and now he was rather peckish.

'Yum, yum,' said the T rex. 'You all look delicious. I am going to **CHOMP** you all up!'

Oh no! Being eaten was one of Wilf's fears. And now it was going to happen! Wilf went all hot. And his ears went all faint. And he felt sick but just in his nose. And his knees wanted to bend the wrong way. He clutched his T-rex toy with one hand and took out his **'HOW TO STOP WORRYING'** leaflet with his other hand. **Number Two** said:

2) Imagine your worry is a monster and then try to describe it. This can actually help your fear become less scary.

Wilf gulped. The T rex took a step closer. Wilf imagined his worry might look a bit like a dinosaur.

T rex took a step closer.

It might well look like a very tall dinosaur.

T rex took a step closer.

It might look like a very tall dinosaur with a massive tail.

T rex took a step closer.

It might look like a very tall dinosaur with a massive tail and enormous jaws.

T rex took a step closer.

It might look like a very tall dinosaur with a massive tail, enormous jaws and huge pointy teeth.

T rex took a step closer. Wilf could feel his breath on his face.

It might look like a very tall dinosaur with a massive tail, enormous jaws, huge pointy teeth and stinky breath.

This actually wasn't helping at all! Instead of standing there describing his fear, he should have been running away very fast!

'Run!' shouted Wilf, scooping up Dot. They all turned and ran as fast as they could. But the T rex was faster. It reached down and snatched Dot out of Wilf's arms and held on to her by the tail of her T-rex costume.

'RARRRRRRRRR!' said Dot.

The T rex looked a bit shocked.

'RARRRR?'

he said.

'RAARRRRRRRRRRRR!' roared Dot.
'**RARRR!**' gasped the T rex.
'**RAARRRRRRRRR RAAARRRRRRRRRR RAARRRRR!**' roared Dot.
'**ROHHHH!**' said the T rex sheepishly.
'**RAAAAAAARRRRRRRRRRRRR!**' roared Dot ferociously.
'**ROOPS,**' gulped the T rex.

He looked a bit scared and quickly put Dot back down on the ground.

'Sorry!' he said.

Then T rex picked up Henry VIII.

'Don't even think about eating me,' bellowed Henry. 'If you try, you will regret it because I will chop your head o—'

But before he could finish, T rex had popped Henry VIII in his mouth. He started to chew but his teeth clanked against Henry's armour.

'PHATTOOOEEEE!'

T rex said, spitting him out again.

Then he picked up Wilf and held him over his gaping mouth. Wilf screamed and clutched his T-rex toy even more tightly. But just as T rex was about to drop Wilf into his mouth and **CHOMP** him up, he stopped.

'Awwwwwwwww! Sweet! I want one!' said T rex.

Wilf opened his eyes and looked round, confused.

'T-rex teddy!' said T rex.

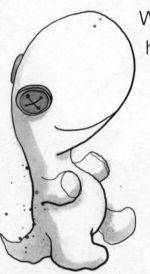

Wilf looked at the cuddly toy under his arm. He held it out.

'Y-y-y-you can h-h-h-ave it if you p-p-p-romise n-n-not to e-e-e-eat m-m-me!' trembled Wilf.

'OK!' said T rex, dropping Wilf and hugging the tiny T-rex teddy with his little arms.

'And look!' said Wilf, having an idea. 'I've got a book too! Full of pictures of you and all your friends!'

The T rex gasped with delight.

'You can have it,' said Wilf. 'But only if you don't eat any of us and you help us mend our **Time Machine Thingy** too.'

'All right,' said T rex. 'Deal.'

And Wilf and T rex shook on it.

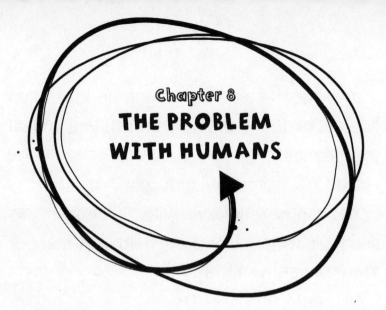

Chapter 8
THE PROBLEM
WITH HUMANS

Wilf, Dot, Stuart, Kevin Phillips and the T Rex
(whose name was Terry) all stared at the **Time
Machine Thingy's** manual, trying to work
out how to fix it.

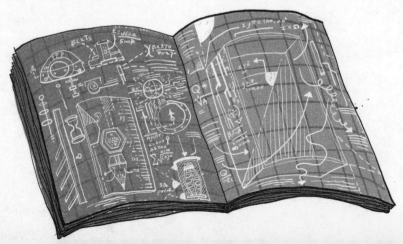

Terry sighed a big sigh, blowing Stuart several metres into the air. Wilf caught him and popped him back in his pocket for safekeeping.

'The problem is,' said Terry, 'I have a small brain. I'm no good at this kind of thing.'

'Nonsense,' said Wilf. 'I bet you're very good at this kind of thing. And even if you're not, you're probably good at other things. We can't all be good at everything,' said Wilf.

'I'm not good at anything. Apart from eating,' said Terry sadly.

'That's just not true. I've only known you a few minutes and I already know that you are very good at roaring, you're very good at running and you're very good at **CHOMPING**. Those are very important things to be good at,' said Wilf.

'RARRRRRR!' agreed Dot.

Terry smiled. 'Do you think so?' he asked.

'I *know* so,' said Wilf.

Just then another dinosaur stomped over.

'Maybe Theo could help?' suggested Terry.

'THERIZINOSAURUS!' shouted Dot, thrilled to bits.

'She can say my name!' said Theo. 'Hardly anyone can say my name. I can't even say my name. That's why I call myself Theo.'

'Pleased to meet you, Theo,' said Wilf politely.

'RARRRRRRR!' said Dot loudly.

'Aaaaah!' screamed Theo. 'Who is she? What does she want? What's wrong? What's happened? Is she going to eat us?' said Theo anxiously, jumping into Terry's arms.

'RARRRRRRRR!' said Dot excitedly.

'She won't eat you,' Wilf assured Theo. 'Don't worry.'

'Don't worry, he says! Don't worry! I can't help it. I *do* worry. I worry all the time. I'm of a nervous disposition. Plus there are big dinosaurs who want to eat me. There are volcanoes erupting all over the place. It's hard not to worry,' said Theo.

'CLAWS?' shouted Dot in a questioning voice, pointing at Theo's hands.

'I know, I know. It's a terrible habit. My claws are meant to be a metre long but I bite them down to stumps. I can't help it. It's a nervous habit.'

'I have something that might be able to help,' said Wilf, handing Theo one of his '**HOW TO STOP WORRYING**' leaflets.

'Thank you, thank you. That's very kind.'

Wilf and Terry explained to Theo that they were trying to fix the **Time Machine Thingy**.

'You know who would be great at this? Annie!' said Theo.

'Yes! Annie is really clever. We need Annie. Where's Annie?' called Terry.

'Over here,' said a big rock.

'Come on, Annie, come out. Don't hide. We need you,' said Theo.

A big lumpy bumpy dinosaur peeked out from behind the rock.

'I don't want them to see me!' squeaked Annie.

'Why not?' asked Wilf.

'I'm covered in lumps and bumps and I have a big fat heavy tail and short legs and a big tummy…'

'ANKYLOSAURUS!' yelled Dot, jumping up and down and clapping.

'I think you're beautiful!' said Wilf.

'Really?' said Annie.

'Not just beautiful. But majestic. And magnificent. And strong.'

'Really?' said Annie.

'Yes,' said Wilf. 'Who said legs have to be long or tummies have to be small? I think you look wonderful!'

Annie beamed. 'Thank you!' she said.

'You're actually my favourite dinosaur,' whispered Wilf.

'And you're my favourite... Erm, what exactly are you?' asked Annie.

'They're big sausagey things with legs,' explained Terry.

'We're called humans,' added Wilf. 'We're just visiting and we need to get home.'

'Well I think you might be my very favourite

creature,' said Annie.

'I don't think you'd say that if you met us all,' said Wilf, at which point they were interrupted by a very loud **SHOUTY** noise. It was Alan and Henry.

'Hello, dinosaurs!' said Alan, striding towards them. **'I, King Alan, as your ruler, shall henceforth rename you. You are Alanosaurus rex, you are Triceralan, you are Alanceratops, you are Alanraptor...'** said Alan, pointing at each of them with his pointy little finger.

'No!' thundered Henry. **'I, King Henry, as your ruler, shall henceforth rename you. You are now Henrysaurus rex, you are Tricerahenry, you are Henryceratops, you are Henryraptor...'**

'Oh do shut up,' said Alan. 'I was here first.'

'And then,' bellowed Henry, 'once I have renamed you, I will invent a tax on having scales and green bodies and big swishy tails and then I shall be rich! Rich I tell you! And I shall use my money to start more wars!'

Terry and Theo and Annie all stared at Alan and Henry, open-jawed with horror.

'Yeeeeeesss… Sorry about them,' said Wilf. 'That's why we need to fix this **Time Machine Thingy**. Then I can take them home.'

Chapter 9
HANG ON, BOOKS HAVEN'T ACTUALLY BEEN INVENTED YET SO HOW ARE YOU READING THIS?

Well, I don't know how many times you've had to fix your **Time Machine Thingy**, but I'm sure you know that it is not an easy thing to do.

And it was even more difficult a squillion million years ago because there were no tools, and no shops to buy tools, and no shops to buy cakes or biscuits or sweets either (which are very good for helping you think).

Alan and Henry were no help. They were off somewhere arguing about who was the tallest or who could run the fastest or who was best at arm wrestling or paper-scissor-stone. So Wilf and Dot and Stuart and their new friends were left trying to fix the blinking thing all on their own.

'What we need,' said Wilf, 'is some wood and some nails to fix the outside of the **Time Machine Thingy**.'

'Well, I've got some wood,' said Terry, ripping up a tree from the ground with one strong little arm (the T-rex toy was tucked under the other arm, of course).

'Great! But where can we get nails?' said Wilf.

Wilf heard a tiny cough in his ear. It was Stuart. Stuart had had an idea. He whispered it to Wilf.

'Yes of course!' said Wilf. 'We can use your dinosaur pencil sharpener to sharpen sticks and use them as nails!'

Dot and Terry and Theo and Annie gathered as many sticks as they could. It took a while, because every time they brought a stick for Wilf to sharpen, Kevin Phillips barked and ran off with it.

Eventually they had collected about twelve sticks (and Kevin Philips had run off with about ninety-eight). Wilf carefully sharpened them all.

'The problem is,' said Wilf, 'that now we

need a hammer. And they haven't been invented yet.'

'Why don't we use my tail?' asked Annie.

'Brilliant!' said Wilf. 'Of course!'

Terry nibbled the tree to the right size, then Terry and Theo held the wood in place, while Wilf and Annie hammered the wooden nails through it. It wasn't long before the outside of the **Time Machine Thingy** was all mended.

But the next bit was trickier. The steering wheel of the **Time Machine Thingy**, which was the big metal globe with levers, was all smushed and broken.

'Oh dear,' said Wilf. 'Where on prehistoric Earth are we going to get some metal?'

At that moment, there was a thundering of feet and a loud yell. They looked round.

Wilf couldn't believe it. Alan and Henry were jousting! Alan was sitting on top of a triceratops (or alanceratops) and Henry was sitting on top of a brachyceratops (or henryceratops) and they were galumphing towards each other at top speed, holding very long tree branches pointed at each other.

'I'm the king of the world,' shouted Alan.

'No, I'm the king of the woooooorld,' bellowed Henry as Alan's stick caught him square in the stomach and he fell off his dinosaur with a loud CLANG.

'Henry's armour!' said Wilf. 'It's made of metal! We need to get it off him!'

Wilf, Dot, Terry, Theo and Annie all strolled up to Henry, whistling nonchalantly and trying to look casual.

'Lovely day, isn't it?' said Wilf. 'Hot. Very hot. Far too hot to be wearing armour. Want me to hang up your armour for you?'

'No, thanks. I'm fine,' bellowed Henry, getting up and dusting himself off.

Drat, thought Wilf.

'Oh dear. You're a bit dusty,' said Wilf. 'Want me to polish your armour for you? You could take it off and I could give it a jolly good polish. Get it gleaming.'

'I'm a bit busy at the moment,' thundered Henry, **'defeating my enemies and being ruler of the world.'**

Double drat, thought Wilf.

'Oh I see,' said Wilf. 'Good luck with that.'

'What do you mean?' hollered Henry.

'Well, I always thought you were the bravest and strongest king but it seems like it must be Alan after all,' said Wilf.

'What did you say, boy?' bellowed Henry. **'And answer quickly while you still have a head on that neck,'** thundered Henry.

Wilf gulped.

'Well, it's just that you're wearing all that armour and Alan isn't wearing any armour at all. So that makes him braver and stronger than you.'

'Absolute poppycock!' roared Henry, struggling out of his armour. **'I'll take my armour off if you don't believe me!**

And the helmet you gave me! And my clothes! And my pants!'

'Probably best to leave your pants on,' said Wilf quickly, covering Dot's eyes. 'But wow, yes, that is very impressive. You must be the bravest and strongest after all.'

'Definitely,' said Theo and Annie.

'What are pants?' said Terry.

'Don't worry about that now,' said Wilf, 'we've got work to do!'

Luckily Henry's armour was already pretty round because of his big tummy. But after Annie had hammered it with her tail, it was almost a perfect globe.

Then Terry used his sharp teeth to tear Henry's shield into strips for the levers.

'Now all we need is a big handle for the main lever,' said Wilf. 'Something big and round. Where will we find something big and round that we can fit on the end of the lever?'

Everyone thought very hard. Everyone paced. Everyone frowned. Everyone scratched their chins.

Suddenly Stuart had an idea.

He hopped up and down with excitement (not easy when you have fourteen legs) and he pointed to the river. Unfortunately he pointed with the leg he was hopping on so he fell over, but then he was straight back up again, hopping and pointing.

'What is it, Stuart?' asked Wilf. 'You want to go to the river?'

Wilf carried his friend to the edge of the river and put him on the ground. Stuart ran as fast as his tiny legs would carry him (i.e. not very fast at all) towards an isopod.

Stuart and the isopod did a series of complicated woodlouse greetings – high fives, low fives, fist bumps and bottom wiggles.

Then Stuart whispered something to his great great great (great times a million) granny and she nodded and dived into the water.

Wilf, Dot, Stuart, Kevin Phillips and their new friends stared at the water and waited.

After a few moments, Granny Isopod swam to the surface holding a big shell.

'Ammonite!' shouted Dot excitedly. 'Pwitty,' she added.

'That's perfect!' said Wilf. 'That shell will make a perfect handle for the lever. Well done, Stuart!'

Stuart smiled and blushed.

Wilf attached the ammonite shell to the top of the lever with his dinosaur chewing gum.

'I think we've done it!' said Wilf excitedly. He tentatively pulled the big lever.

Nothing happened.

He pulled it again.

Nothing.

He pulled it again.

Nope. Nothing.

Everyone sighed, accidentally blowing all the leaves off a nearby tree.

'There must be something broken inside the control panel. But that's closed with screws and we don't have a screwdriver,' said Wilf, beginning to despair.

'Well, since you helped me stop worrying, I've stopped biting my claws so much, and they've grown a little bit,' said Theo. 'Maybe I could use those!'

Theo put one of his claws into the head of the screws and slowly unscrewed it. Then he did the same for the other screws.

They took away the panel. Inside was a big mess of tiny wires. But Wilf could see that one or two had come loose. What were they going to do? His hands were too big to fit inside and Theo and Annie and Terry's hands were MUCH MUCH MUCH too big. In fact, even Dot's sticky little mitts were too big.

'Hmm,' said Wilf. 'This is going to be tricky. Anybody got any ideas?'

There was a long silence while everyone thought again. They were still mid-thunk when the silence was interrupted—

'*Doo doo doo, diddly doo.*'

It was Stuart.

'*Doo doo doo, diddly doo.*'

He was humming the
Superman theme tune.

'*Doodly doo doo, doodly doo doo...*'

He was humming the Superman theme tune and tying the yo-yo string around his waist.

'Doodly diddly dum, de dum de dum.'

'Stuart! You're a genius!' said Wilf. He took the yo-yo and began to lower Stuart into the control panel. 'Be careful now!' Wilf added.

Stuart stopped to salute Wilf, then Wilf continued lowering him down.

Once inside, Stuart could see that a wire was broken and frayed. He hauled one half of the broken wire with all his might (which was actually not that much might) towards the other half and then, using all fourteen of his legs, he plaited the two broken ends together.

He gave a whistle and tugged two times on the yo-yo string and Wilf slowly wound the yo-yo up, pulling Stuart out.

'Doo doo doo, diddly doo,' hummed Stuart. 'Doo doo doo, diddly doo.'

He was pretty pleased with himself.

'Doodly doo doo, doodly doo doo...'

Sometimes it's good to be a woodlouse.

'Doodly diddly dum, de dum de dum.'

'Well done, Stuart! You are so brave!' said Wilf, and he gave Stuart a chocolate sprinkle he'd been saving for just such an occasion.

Theo screwed the lid of the control panel back into place. The **Time Machine Thingy** hummed into life.

'Wahooo!' whooped Wilf and his dinosaur friends. They all high-fived each other.

'You see, Terry?' said Wilf. 'You *are* good

at this sort of thing. I think that actually your brain must be jolly big.'

Wilf handed Terry the book about dinosaurs and Terry smiled a big toothy grin.

Suddenly there was another loud shout.

'Take that you puny worm!'

It was Henry. He had bent a big bendy tree right back so the top reached right to the ground. Then he had heaved a huge boulder on to the top of the tree.

'I am not a puny worm!' shouted Alan. **'I am King Alan, ruler of the world,'** and to prove his point, he revealed a throne he had fashioned out of some branches with a sign above it saying, **'Ruler of the World'**.

'Oh no you're not!' bellowed Henry.

'Oh yes I am!' said Alan.

'Oh no you're not!' said Henry and he let

go of the tree which went *ba-doinging* upwards, hurling the boulder towards Alan. Alan yelped and leapt out of the way, but the boulder landed right on Alan's throne, smashing it to bits.

'Not again,' sighed Wilf. He turned back to the dinosaurs. 'Well, thanks to you, I can go home now,' said Wilf. 'And I can take those two with me and leave you in peace,' he added. He opened the door of the **Time Machine Thingy**.

Just then, Alan raced straight past him and through the door, slamming it behind him. A second later, the **Time Machine Thingy** disappeared into thin air.

Wilf and Dot and Henry were left behind. The only humans on planet Earth!

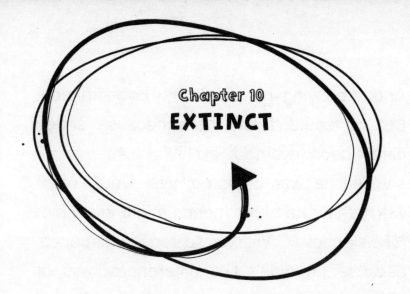

Chapter 10
EXTINCT

Wilf felt hot and cold and faint and he felt sick, not just in one place but EVERYWHERE. And his knees were going the wrong way and his tummy hurt and he was so scared and homesick. He sobbed and sobbed and he sobbed so much that Terry offered to give him his cuddly T-rex toy back. But that wouldn't help! Nothing would help! The only thing that would help was to be at home.

And to be lying in his bed. Or maybe knitting. But he couldn't knit here because sheep hadn't been invented yet!

When he was at home, Wilf would often worry that one of his friends might invite him for a sleepover. Wilf was scared of sleepovers because he didn't like different pillows or being away for the night or using a different loo. And also because other people's houses smell different and make different noises. And because he always got a tummy ache because he missed his bed and his toys.

But this was much worse than staying at someone's house for ONE NIGHT. This was staying somewhere FOREVER. Somewhere that didn't have ANY pillows or houses or beds or toys.

Wilf sobbed so much that he worried his

eyes might run out of tears. His new friends tried very hard to cheer him up. Terry showed him his dinosaur book and told him the names of all his friends that he found in it. Annie stroked him gently with her tail. And Theo paced around anxiously reading his '**HOW TO STOP WORRYING**' leaflet.

Meanwhile Dot was happily shouting, '**RARRRRRRRRRRRR!**' because she didn't understand what had happened. And in the background Henry was yelling, '**I win! I am the kingiest king ever. I am the king of the whole wide world!**' And then he did a little dance because he was really rather good at dancing.

'Wilf?' said Theo. 'It says in the leaflet you gave me that doing yoga can help if you are worried or scared. Shall we try doing that?'

Wilf nodded, although the last thing he felt like doing was yoga. In fact he didn't really want to do anything that wasn't crying or sobbing in a rather snotty way.

Nevertheless he tried his very hardest to do downward dog, which is a special yoga move where you stick your bottom in the air. Theo and Wilf and Dot and Kevin Phillips were all sticking their bottoms in the air when suddenly they heard a loud wail.

It was Terry. He had just reached the end of the dinosaur book.

'What does EXTINCT mean?' wailed Terry. 'And what's a METEOR?' he cried.

'That's actually one of my worries,' said Theo. 'I always used to worry that a HUGE METEOR would fall out of the sky and crash into Earth and we would all be killed. But that's just silly.'

They all turned to look at Wilf.

'Isn't it?'

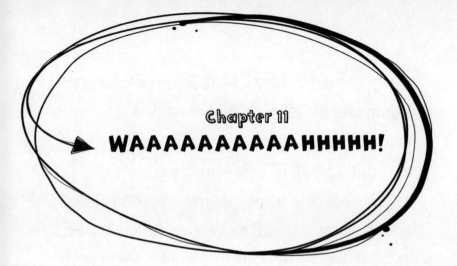

Chapter 11

WAAAAAAAAAAHHHHH!

Now Wilf was crying and all the dinosaurs were crying and Kevin Phillips was crying because Dot was pulling his tail. It was a very sad sight.

'Think I might treat myself to a seventh wife,' thundered Henry, as he jigged past. **'Where will I find myself one of those?'**

'There aren't any,' said Wilf. 'Not for another squillion gazillion years.'

At which point Henry burst into tears, too.

'Waaaaaaahhhhhhhhhh,' bawled Henry.

'Boo hoo, sob sob, sniff sniff,' cried everyone else.

'WAAAAAAAAHHHHHH,' cried Terry.

In fact they were making so much noise, they didn't hear the strange sort of whirry zoomy splodgy sound right behind them.

Suddenly Kevin Phillips gave a bark and wagged his tail and they looked round to see the **Time Machine Thingy**! The door opened and Alan shuffled out.

Everybody was happier to see Alan than they could ever have imagined they would be.

'Alan!' they cried with delight. 'We're saved!'

'Look what I went to get from home!' said Alan, ignoring them. 'The **biggiest gunniest thing ever**!' he said proudly, hauling out what was indeed the **Biggest Gunniest Thing Ever**.

'If I can't be king of the world then I'm going to destroy the world — almost before it's begun! Ha ha ha ha! That'll show all those people who haven't even been born yet!'

'Oh no!' said Wilf. 'Maybe we're a bit less saved than we thought.'

Alan and Kevin started dragging the **Biggest Gunniest Thing Ever** up the nearest volcano.

'Do I have permission to eat them now?' asked Terry.

'No, that wouldn't be right,' said Wilf. 'But we must do something!'

Theo got out his '**HOW TO STOP WORRYING**' leaflet again. 'It says here that it can help to think up a battle cry when you are facing frightening situations.'

'Good idea!' said Wilf. 'A battle cry. Yes. Let's think of a battle cry.'

'How about, "Heeeeeeeeeeeeeeeeeelp"?' suggested Theo.

'Or just, "Meeeeeeeeeeeep"?' said Wilf.

'Or, "Yikes"?' said Theo.

'Or we could try "Noooooooooo"', said Wilf.

'Or maybe, "We'reallgoingtodiewe'reallgoin gtodiewe'reallgoingto die!"', suggested Theo.

'Is this helping at all?' asked Wilf.

'Not really,' said Theo.

'I think it might actually be making it worse,' said Wilf. 'We need to find a way to stop Alan!'

'Easy,' said Terry. 'If I can't **CHOMP** him, I'll stomp on him.'

'That probably *is* the best plan,' admitted Wilf. 'But try not to make him too splatty. Just splatted enough to stop him from destroying the world.'

Terry nodded and started thundering up the volcano towards Alan. Wilf and Theo and Annie and Dot were cheering Terry on and he was about half way there when Wilf was shoved aside by Henry.

'You're not going to destroy the world!' bellowed Henry to Alan. 'Because I, King Henry, am going to stop you!'

And with that he bent another tree backwards, hauled the biggiest rockiest boulder on to it and let go of the tree.

The boulder went flying up into the air…

and fell on Terry, knocking him to the ground.

'Terry!' Wilf gasped.

'You were meant to hit Alan!' said Theo.

'That was a terrible shot!' said Annie.

'You sound just like my sixth wife,' grumbled Henry.

Wilf and Dot and Theo and Annie ran over to Terry, who was lying on the ground, groaning.

'Are you all right?' asked Annie.

'Where does it hurt?' said Wilf.

'This is all terrible,' said Theo, gnawing his nails again.

'Rarrr,' said Dot sadly.

'Owwwww,' said Terry. 'My head!'

A big green egg-shaped lump had appeared on it.

Wilf was scared. What were they going to do? Someone had to stop Alan! And now

Terry was hurt, it was going to have to be Wilf. He didn't have time to panic. Though there was nothing he would have liked more than to have a great big old panic. Or a great big old worry. Or a lovely long hide under the duvet. But he couldn't. It was just Wilf. Wilf against Alan. The future of the whole world depended on it. If Wilf didn't do something, the world was going to end, almost before it had begun!

'You look after Terry,' said Wilf to his friends. 'I'm going to stop Alan.'

Wilf started running up the volcano as fast as his little legs would carry him. He ran like a cheetah on roller skates. He ran like a dog chasing a sausage. He ran like a hare with its tail on fire. He ran and he ran and he ran and he ran.

At the top of the volcano, Alan and Kevin Phillips were hauling the **Biggiest Gunniest Thing Ever** into place.

'Right,' said Alan. 'Take aim and faaaaaaa...' he shrieked as Wilf hurled himself at Alan, knocking him to the ground.

Wilf grabbed the **Biggiest Gunniest Thing Ever** and started running away with it. It was ever so heavy, but that didn't stop Wilf. He ran and ran. He ran until his ears hurt and his eyes watered and his lungs felt like they would pop.

Alan and Kevin chased after him, getting closer and closer, catching him up, catching him up, **catchinghimup** until suddenly – **WADOOMPH!** – Wilf tripped over Kevin and the gun went FLYING through the air.

Wilf crawled towards it but Alan grabbed him. Wilf and Alan tussled and grappled and scuffled and scrapped and brawled and fought. And finally, Alan wrestled the **Biggiest Gunniest Thing Ever** from Wilf's hands.

'And now I shall prove that I am the biggiest baddiest baddie in the whole wide world EVER in history by destroying the world and then you shall all be dead. **Deadity deadity deadingtons. Deadity deadity doobery doo doo. A deadity deadity deadity— Eh?'**

As Alan was speaking, it suddenly went very, very dark.

They all looked up to see a HUGE METEOR plummeting towards them. It was travelling at about a kerbillion miles an hour, getting bigger and bigger as it got closer and closer.

Everybody screamed. 'Aaaaaaaah! We're all going to die!'

'Yes,' said Alan impatiently. 'That's the exact point I was making.'

'Aaaaaaaaah! It's the end! It's the end!'

'At last! People are taking me seriously!' said Alan happily. 'This is what I've been waiting for.'

'The METEOR is going to kill us!'

'Yes,' said Alan. 'No. Wait. What? I'm going to kill you!'

'The METEOR! Aaaaah! The METEOR!' screamed everybody, ignoring Alan.

'Forget about the stupid METEOR. I, Alan am going to kill you. ME. The biddly boddly baddest man in the whole wide worlderoony.'

And as he spoke, Alan put his finger on the trigger.

'Prepare to DIE!' yelled Alan.

'Eek!' said Alan, jumping out of his skin and falling backwards over Kevin.

And as he fell, he pressed the trigger and fired the **Biggiest Bullietist Bullet Ever** out of the **Biggiest Gunniest Thing Ever.**

The bullet went hurtling up into the sky and

into the centre of the METEOR, shattering it and obliterating it into a million obliterations which burned and fizzed in the atmosphere like a thousand tiny fireworks.

'Hooray!' shouted everyone, jumping up and down with delight.

'What happened?' said Alan scrambling to his feet and looking round, dazed and confused.

'You saved the world!' said Wilf, giving Alan a great big happy hug.

'I did what?' said Alan, horrified.

'YOU SAVED THE WORLD!' shouted everyone happily.

'Drat!' said Alan. 'I wanted to destroy the world! Why doesn't anything ever work out for me?' he wailed.

But his wailing was muffled by Annie and Theo and Terry (whose head was feeling much better) all giving him great big hugs and great big slobbery dinosaur kisses.

'That was a blooming good shot,' thundered Henry, stepping forward. 'I couldn't have done that. I would have missed by a mile. So I suppose you are king of the world after all.' Henry lifted the crown from his head and placed it on Alan's head.

Everyone cheered and the dinosaurs lifted Alan up and carried him on their shoulders.

'You are my hero!' shouted Wilf to Alan happily.

And even Alan couldn't help smiling.

Chapter 12
ALAN HAS SAVED THE WORLD!

Wilf and Alan and Kevin Phillips said goodbye to the dinosaurs.

Dot said **'RARRRRRR!'** to the dinosaurs (terrifying several of them) and they all climbed back into the **Time Machine Thingy**.

They stopped in 1546 to drop Henry off at Hampton Court Palace.

'Pop back and have a game of tennis

some time,' bellowed Henry, as he and Alan hugged each other goodbye.

Then, at last, they arrived back in the present. Wilf and Dot and Stuart rushed into their house.

'You've got your shoes on the wrong feet,' said Wilf's mum, looking up briefly from her newspaper.

Stuart scuttled to his matchbox where he curled up and fell straight to sleep after all his adventures.

Wilf hurried to his lovely cosy bed with his special pillow, surrounded by all his toys. He lay down and sighed a happy sigh.

Dot clambered into her cot and jumped up and down with delight. 'Tee hee! Tee hee!' she giggled, pointing out of the window.

Wilf sat up and looked out into the garden. And there he saw the most **STAGGERBLASTING** sight.

Dinosaurs!

Lots of them! Grazing in their garden. And in Alan's garden. And in all the gardens.

'But…' began Wilf. 'But how did they get here…?'

'BOOM!' said Dot.

Wilf looked at Dot, suddenly realizing what had happened. 'Oh my goodness,' said Wilf. 'You're right! We stopped the METEOR. So they didn't become EXTINCT. We rescued the dinosaurs!'

A pterodactyl swooped past and a parasaurolophus sipped water from the pond. A brachiosaur leaned in through the window and chewed on the curtains.

'Uh oh,' said Wilf.

'RARRRR!' said Dot.

THE END

Discover more of Wilf's adventures in these brilliant books!

WILF THE MIGHTY WORRIER

Georgia Pritchett

'A total delight of a, what I call, book.' MIRANDA HART

'A lively, funny story.' JACQUELINE WILSON

SAVES THE WORLD

Wilf meets Alan for the first time, and discovers his new next-door neighbour wants to destroy the world with his Big Gun Thingy!

When Alan decides that pirating is an excellent way to destroy the world, Wilf will have to overcome his fear of parrots and walking the plank to save the day...

...Psst! There's more over the page!

WILF THE MIGHTY WORRIER

Georgia Pritchett

'A total delight of a, what I call, book.'
MIRANDA HART

ILLUSTRATED BY
JAMIE LITTLER

AND THE ALIEN INVASION

Alan is determined to be the most evil man in the whole universe. Destroying Mars is first on his To-Do list. Yes! Wilf's going to space!

wilfthemightyworrier.com